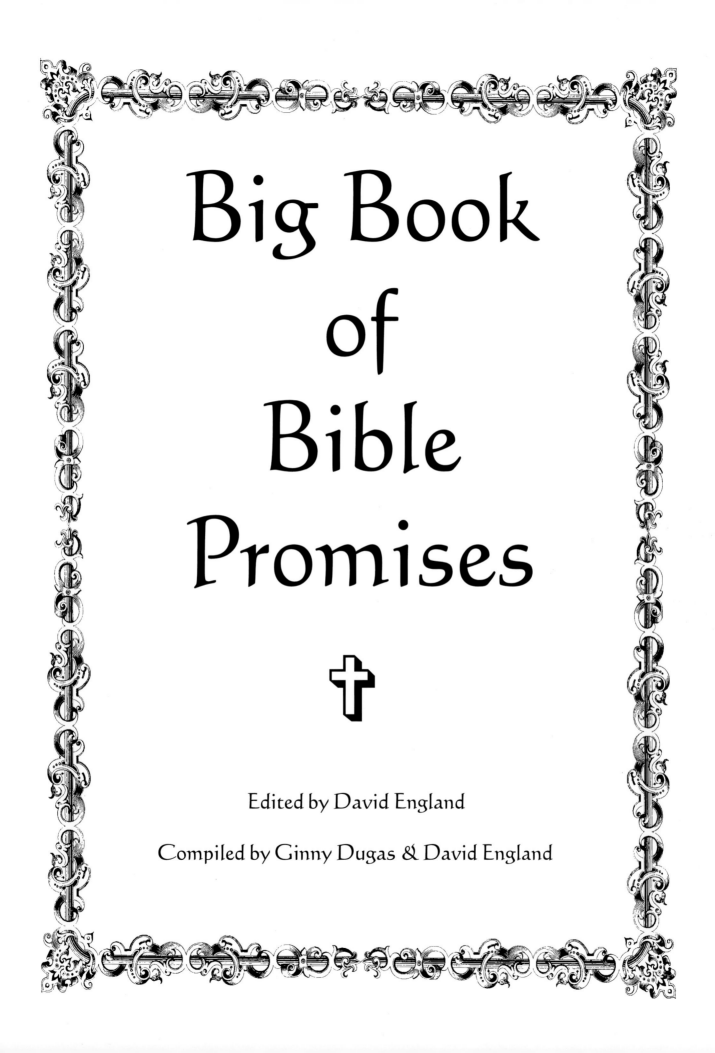

Big Book
of
Bible
Promises

✝

Edited by David England

Compiled by Ginny Dugas & David England

VITAL ISSUES PRESS, INC.
P.O. BOX 53788
LAFAYETTE, LA 70505

Library of Congress Card Catalog Number
96-60919
ISBN 1-56384-123-1

PRINTED IN HONG KONG

All Scripture quotations are taken from the
King James version of the Bible.

CONTENTS

ANGER 7

CHILDREN 9

COMFORT 11

COURAGE 13

FAITH 15

FEAR 17

FORGIVENESS 19

GRACE 21

GUIDANCE 23

HOPE 25

HUMILITY 27

JOY 29

LOVE FOR OTHERS 31

PATIENCE 33

Peace 35

Perseverance 37

Poverty 39

Praise 41

Prayer 43

Pride 45

Protection 47

Salvation 49

Sickness 51

Sin 53

Sorrow 55

Temptation 57

Unity 59

Word of God 61

List of Art & Artists 63

Big Book
of
Bible
Promises

†

LaLutte (Wrestling), Emile Friant, 1889

ANGER

Anger—the feeling one has toward something or someone that hurts, opposes, offends, or annoys; strong displeasure.

God wants you to control your anger. Anger in your heart gives place to the devil. If you give the devil an inch, he'll try to take a mile. Walk in forgiveness toward others, NOT anger.

❖

Wherefore, my beloved brethren, let every man be swift to hear, slow to speak, slow to wrath: For the wrath of man worketh not the righteousness of God.
James 1:19-20

Be not hasty in thy spirit to be angry:
for anger resteth in the bosom of fools.
Ecclesiastes 7:9

For his anger endureth but a moment;
in his favor is life: weeping may endure for a night, but joy comes in the morning.
Psalm 30:5

A soft answer turneth away wrath:
but grievous words stir up anger.
Proverbs 15:1

Detail from *Sunlight*, Frank Benson, 1902

CHILDREN

You are never too small or young for God to use you.
Jesus was only 12 years old when He began to do His Father's work. God
loves you, and He has big plans for your life. He
wants to spend time with you and be your best friend.

❖

I love them that love me;
and those that seek me early shall find me.
Proverbs 8:17

And all thy children shall be taught of the Lord;
and great shall be the peace of thy children.
Isaiah 54:13

Train up a child in the way he should go:
and when he is old, he will not depart from it.
Proverbs 22:6

Children, obey your parents in the Lord, for this
is right . . . That it may be well with thee, and
thou mayest live long on the earth.
Ephesians 6:1,3

Children, obey your parents in all things:
for this is well pleasing unto the Lord.
Colossians 3:20

Mother and Child, J. Alden Weir, 1891

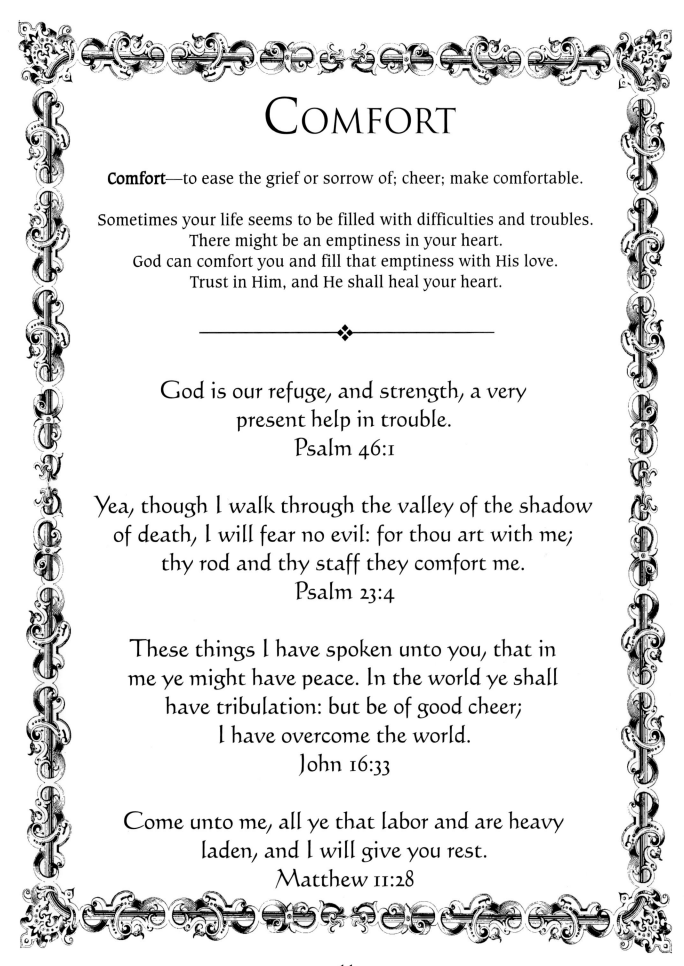

COMFORT

Comfort—to ease the grief or sorrow of; cheer; make comfortable.

Sometimes your life seems to be filled with difficulties and troubles.
There might be an emptiness in your heart.
God can comfort you and fill that emptiness with His love.
Trust in Him, and He shall heal your heart.

❖

God is our refuge, and strength, a very
present help in trouble.
Psalm 46:1

Yea, though I walk through the valley of the shadow
of death, I will fear no evil: for thou art with me;
thy rod and thy staff they comfort me.
Psalm 23:4

These things I have spoken unto you, that in
me ye might have peace. In the world ye shall
have tribulation: but be of good cheer;
I have overcome the world.
John 16:33

Come unto me, all ye that labor and are heavy
laden, and I will give you rest.
Matthew 11:28

Saint George and the Dragon, Raphael, 1504-1505

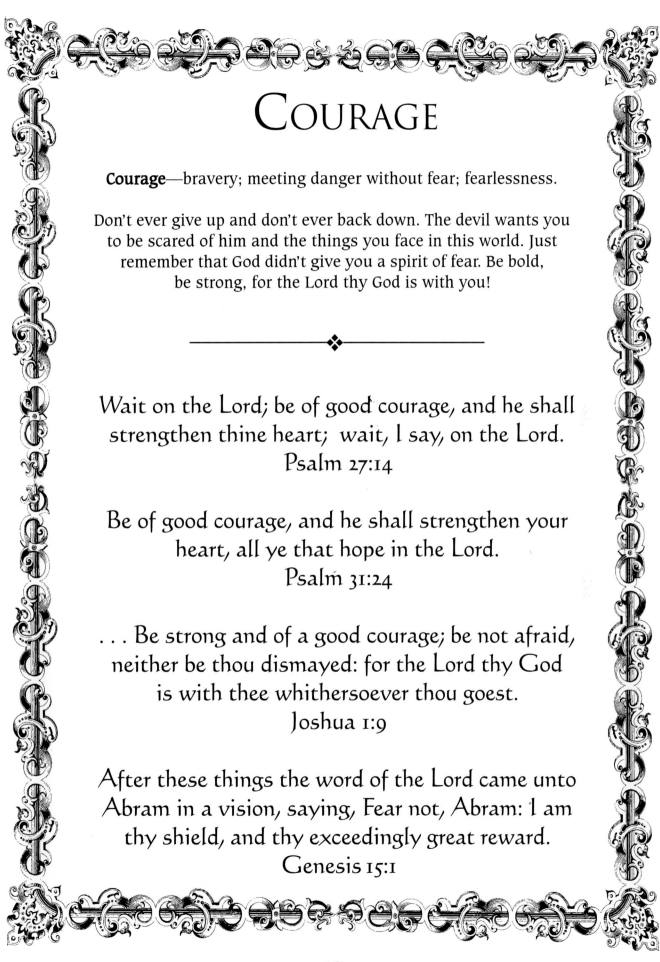

COURAGE

Courage—bravery; meeting danger without fear; fearlessness.

Don't ever give up and don't ever back down. The devil wants you to be scared of him and the things you face in this world. Just remember that God didn't give you a spirit of fear. Be bold, be strong, for the Lord thy God is with you!

❖

Wait on the Lord; be of good courage, and he shall strengthen thine heart; wait, I say, on the Lord.
Psalm 27:14

Be of good courage, and he shall strengthen your heart, all ye that hope in the Lord.
Psalm 31:24

. . . Be strong and of a good courage; be not afraid, neither be thou dismayed: for the Lord thy God is with thee whithersoever thou goest.
Joshua 1:9

After these things the word of the Lord came unto Abram in a vision, saying, Fear not, Abram: I am thy shield, and thy exceedingly great reward.
Genesis 15:1

Detail from *The Angel Stopping Abraham from Sacrificing Isaac to God,* Rembrandt, 1635

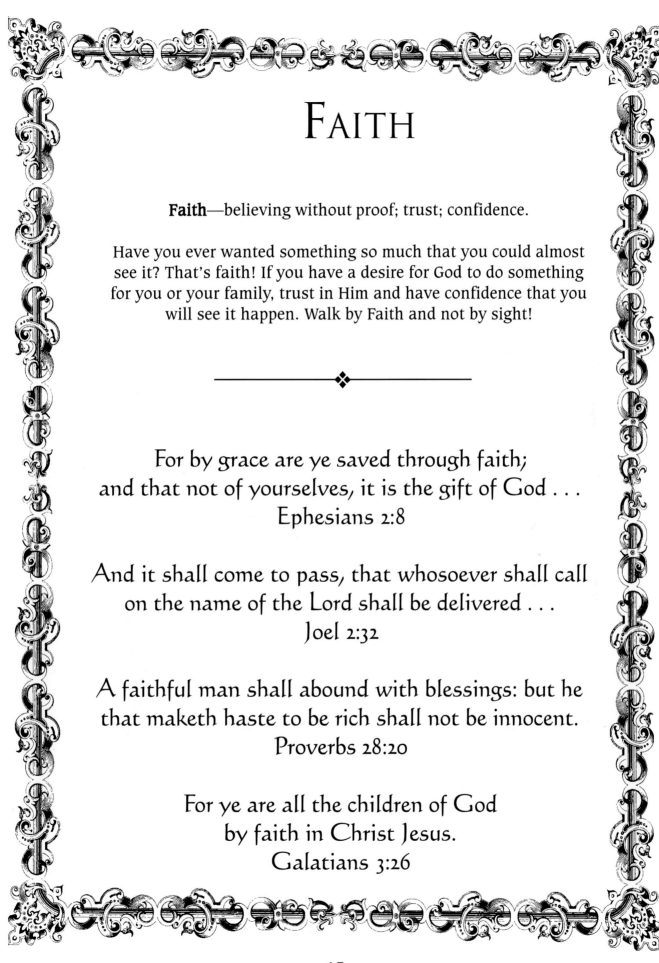

FAITH

Faith—believing without proof; trust; confidence.

Have you ever wanted something so much that you could almost see it? That's faith! If you have a desire for God to do something for you or your family, trust in Him and have confidence that you will see it happen. Walk by Faith and not by sight!

❖

For by grace are ye saved through faith;
and that not of yourselves, it is the gift of God . . .
Ephesians 2:8

And it shall come to pass, that whosoever shall call
on the name of the Lord shall be delivered . . .
Joel 2:32

A faithful man shall abound with blessings: but he
that maketh haste to be rich shall not be innocent.
Proverbs 28:20

For ye are all the children of God
by faith in Christ Jesus.
Galatians 3:26

15

The Fire, Jean-Pierre Alexandre Antigna, 1850

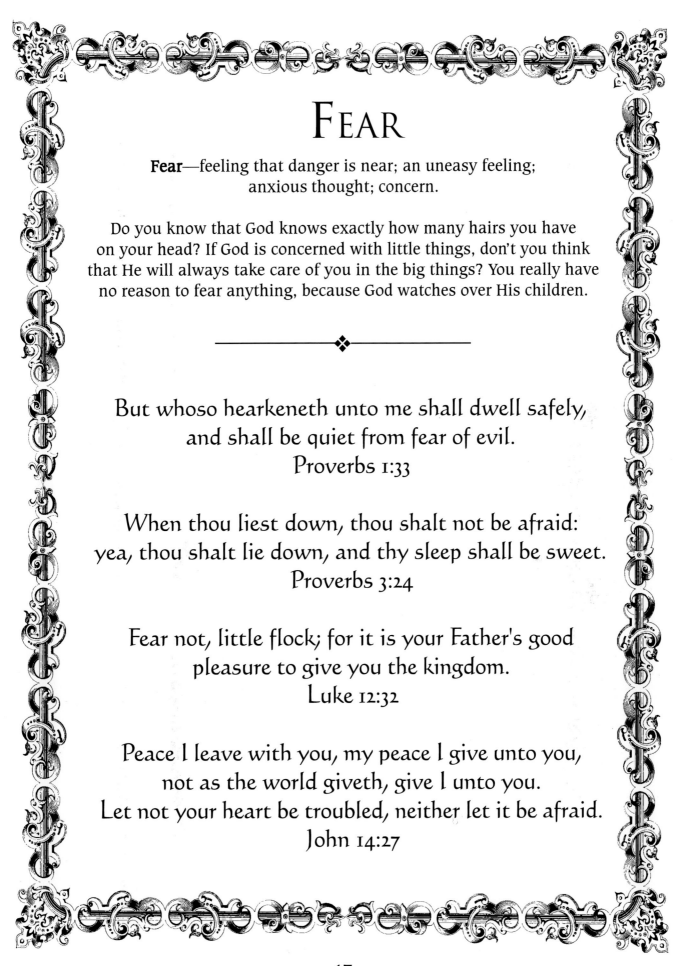

Fear

Fear—feeling that danger is near; an uneasy feeling; anxious thought; concern.

Do you know that God knows exactly how many hairs you have on your head? If God is concerned with little things, don't you think that He will always take care of you in the big things? You really have no reason to fear anything, because God watches over His children.

❖

But whoso hearkeneth unto me shall dwell safely,
and shall be quiet from fear of evil.
Proverbs 1:33

When thou liest down, thou shalt not be afraid:
yea, thou shalt lie down, and thy sleep shall be sweet.
Proverbs 3:24

Fear not, little flock; for it is your Father's good
pleasure to give you the kingdom.
Luke 12:32

Peace I leave with you, my peace I give unto you,
not as the world giveth, give I unto you.
Let not your heart be troubled, neither let it be afraid.
John 14:27

Detail from *The Return of the Prodigal Son,* Rembrandt, 17th Century

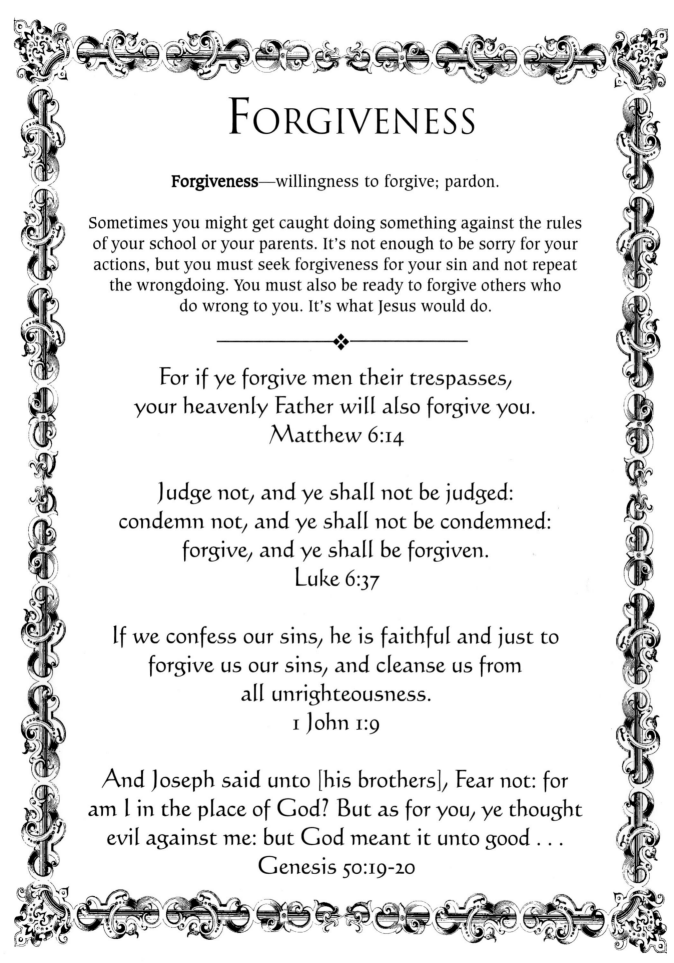

FORGIVENESS

Forgiveness—willingness to forgive; pardon.

Sometimes you might get caught doing something against the rules of your school or your parents. It's not enough to be sorry for your actions, but you must seek forgiveness for your sin and not repeat the wrongdoing. You must also be ready to forgive others who do wrong to you. It's what Jesus would do.

❖

For if ye forgive men their trespasses,
your heavenly Father will also forgive you.
Matthew 6:14

Judge not, and ye shall not be judged:
condemn not, and ye shall not be condemned:
forgive, and ye shall be forgiven.
Luke 6:37

If we confess our sins, he is faithful and just to
forgive us our sins, and cleanse us from
all unrighteousness.
1 John 1:9

And Joseph said unto [his brothers], Fear not: for
am I in the place of God? But as for you, ye thought
evil against me: but God meant it unto good . . .
Genesis 50:19-20

Detail from *The Adoration of the Shepherds,* Giorgione (Venice), circa 1505

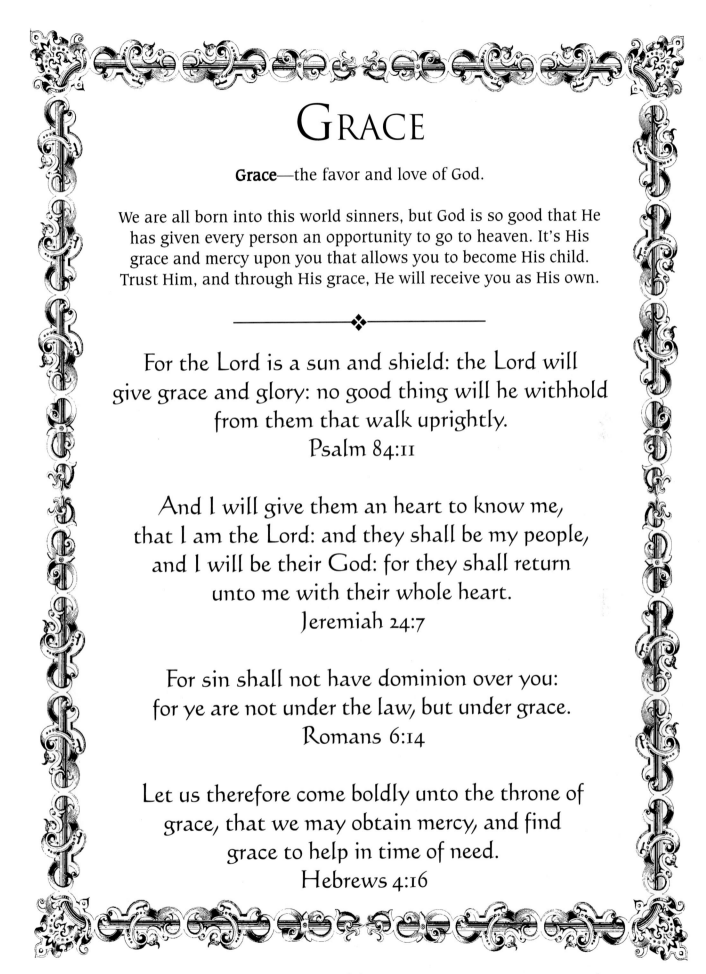

GRACE

Grace—the favor and love of God.

We are all born into this world sinners, but God is so good that He has given every person an opportunity to go to heaven. It's His grace and mercy upon you that allows you to become His child. Trust Him, and through His grace, He will receive you as His own.

❖

For the Lord is a sun and shield: the Lord will give grace and glory: no good thing will he withhold from them that walk uprightly.
Psalm 84:11

And I will give them an heart to know me, that I am the Lord: and they shall be my people, and I will be their God: for they shall return unto me with their whole heart.
Jeremiah 24:7

For sin shall not have dominion over you: for ye are not under the law, but under grace.
Romans 6:14

Let us therefore come boldly unto the throne of grace, that we may obtain mercy, and find grace to help in time of need.
Hebrews 4:16

Detail from *Advice to a Young Artist,* Honoré Daumier, circa 1860

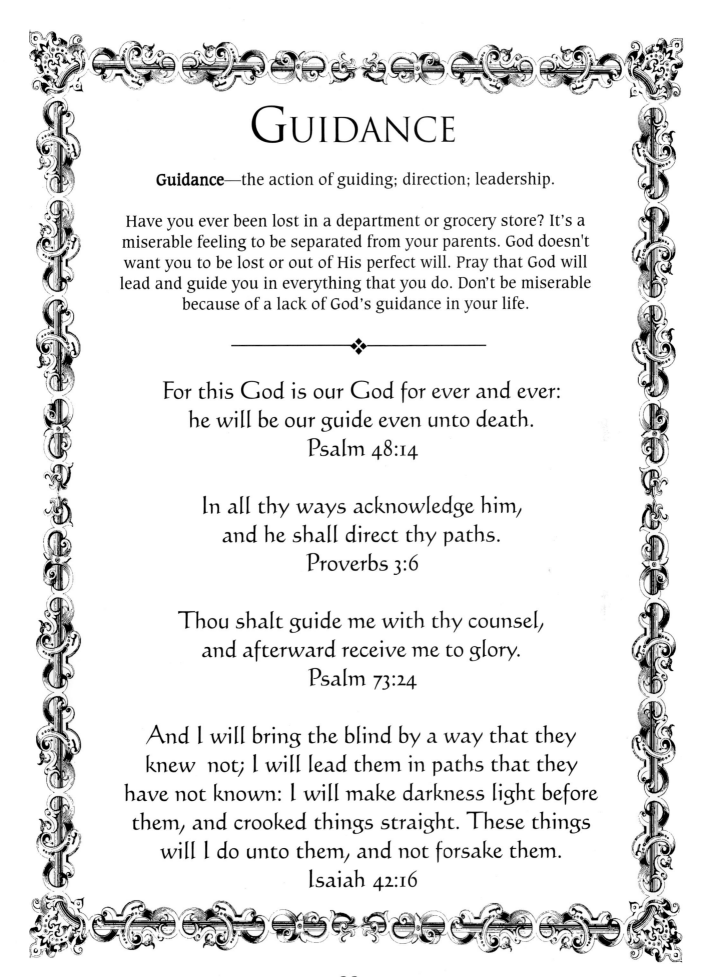

GUIDANCE

Guidance—the action of guiding; direction; leadership.

Have you ever been lost in a department or grocery store? It's a miserable feeling to be separated from your parents. God doesn't want you to be lost or out of His perfect will. Pray that God will lead and guide you in everything that you do. Don't be miserable because of a lack of God's guidance in your life.

❖

For this God is our God for ever and ever:
he will be our guide even unto death.
Psalm 48:14

In all thy ways acknowledge him,
and he shall direct thy paths.
Proverbs 3:6

Thou shalt guide me with thy counsel,
and afterward receive me to glory.
Psalm 73:24

And I will bring the blind by a way that they
knew not; I will lead them in paths that they
have not known: I will make darkness light before
them, and crooked things straight. These things
will I do unto them, and not forsake them.
Isaiah 42:16

Sketch for *Soldiers Distributing Bread,* Isidore Pils, circa 1850

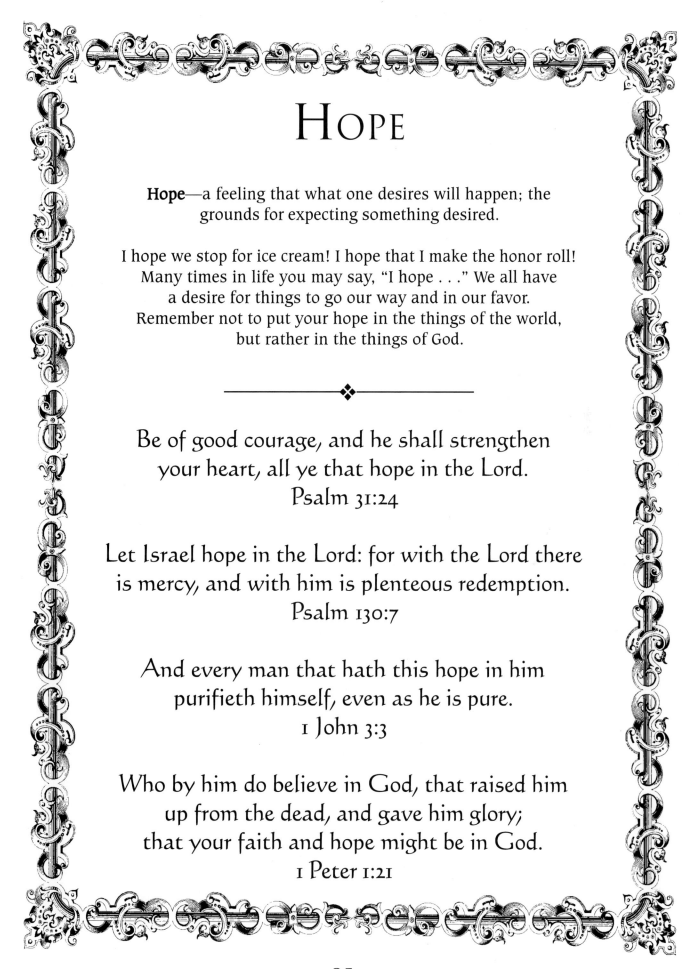

HOPE

Hope—a feeling that what one desires will happen; the grounds for expecting something desired.

I hope we stop for ice cream! I hope that I make the honor roll! Many times in life you may say, "I hope . . ." We all have a desire for things to go our way and in our favor. Remember not to put your hope in the things of the world, but rather in the things of God.

❖

Be of good courage, and he shall strengthen your heart, all ye that hope in the Lord.
Psalm 31:24

Let Israel hope in the Lord: for with the Lord there is mercy, and with him is plenteous redemption.
Psalm 130:7

And every man that hath this hope in him purifieth himself, even as he is pure.
1 John 3:3

Who by him do believe in God, that raised him up from the dead, and gave him glory; that your faith and hope might be in God.
1 Peter 1:21

Holy Family with the Lamb, Raphael, circa 1505

HUMILITY

Humility—lack of pride; meekness.

Guard your mouth! Be careful not to speak of yourself too much in your conversation with your friends. Your friends will like you more if you show interest in them. Listen to people with a sincere heart, and humble yourself; for you will be exalted in due season.

❖

Whosoever therefore shall humble himself as
this little child, the same is greatest in
the kingdom of heaven.
Matthew 18:4

Lord, thou hast heard the desire of the humble:
thou wilt prepare their heart,
thou wilt cause thine ear to hear.
Psalm 10:17

Surely he scorneth the scorners;
but he giveth grace unto the lowly.
Proverbs 3:34

Humble yourselves therefore under the mighty hand
of God, that he may exalt you in due time.
1 Peter 5:6

Detail from *Breezing Up,* Winslow Homer, 1876

JOY

Joy—a glad feeling; strong feeling of pleasure; happiness.

A merry heart doeth good like a medicine. The joy of the Lord is like a "burst of energy." When you feel tired, sick, or down in the dumps, it's time to fill your heart with the joy of the Lord. The joy of the Lord can heal your heart, a friendship, or any situation.

❖

Therefore the redeemed of the Lord shall return, and come with singing into Zion; and everlasting joy shall be upon their head . . .
Isaiah 51:11

But let all those that put their trust in thee rejoice: let them ever shout for joy, because thou defendeth them: let them also that love thy name be joyful in thee.
Psalm 5:11

. . . I will see you again, and your heart shall rejoice, and your joy no man taketh from you.
John 16:22

But rejoice, inasmuch as ye are partakers of Christ's sufferings; that, when his glory shall be revealed, ye may be glad also with exceeding joy.
1 Peter 4:13

The Artist's Family, Renoir, 1896

Love for Others

Love (for others)—fond or tender feeling; warm liking; affection; attachment.

We have all heard the "golden rule" at one time or another: "Do unto others as you would have them do unto you." God commands you to love those around you as you love yourself. You would never tease or ridicule yourself; therefore, you shouldn't behave in that manner toward others. Be kind and walk in Love.

❖

By this shall all men know that ye are my disciples,
if ye have love one to another.
John 13:35

Beloved, let us love one another: for love is of God;
and every one that loveth is born of God,
and knoweth God.
1 John 4:7-8

Finally, be ye all of one mind, having compassion
one of another, love as brethren . . . knowing that ye
are thereunto called, that ye should inherit a blessing.
1 Peter 3:8,9

But to do good and to communicate forget not:
for with such sacrifices God is well pleased.
Hebrews 13:16

The Little Cook, Pierre Edouard Frère, 1858

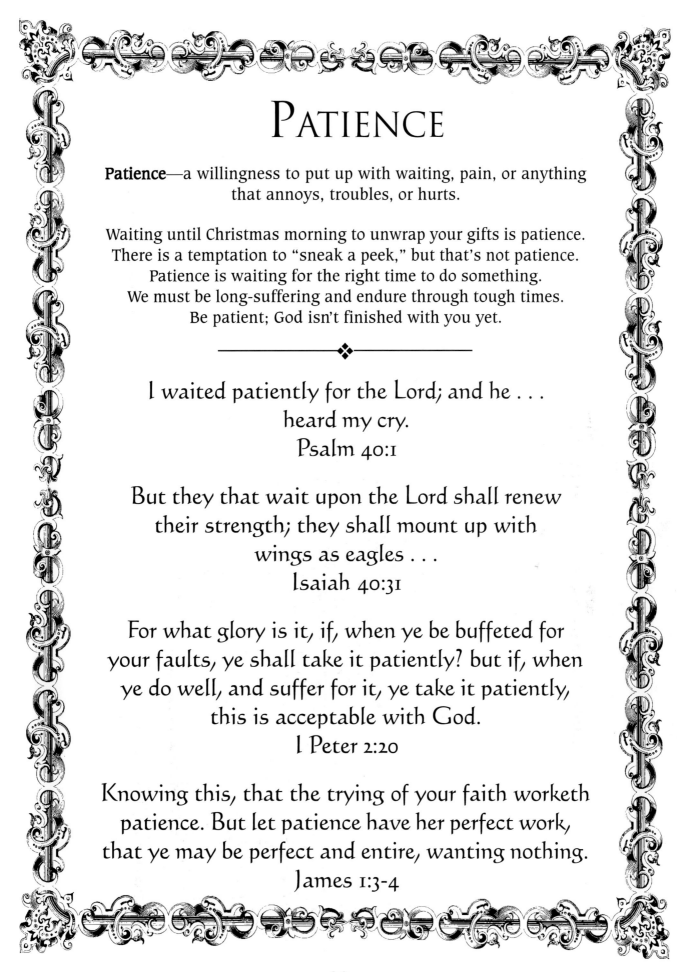

PATIENCE

Patience—a willingness to put up with waiting, pain, or anything that annoys, troubles, or hurts.

Waiting until Christmas morning to unwrap your gifts is patience.
There is a temptation to "sneak a peek," but that's not patience.
Patience is waiting for the right time to do something.
We must be long-suffering and endure through tough times.
Be patient; God isn't finished with you yet.

❖

I waited patiently for the Lord; and he . . .
heard my cry.
Psalm 40:1

But they that wait upon the Lord shall renew
their strength; they shall mount up with
wings as eagles . . .
Isaiah 40:31

For what glory is it, if, when ye be buffeted for
your faults, ye shall take it patiently? but if, when
ye do well, and suffer for it, ye take it patiently,
this is acceptable with God.
1 Peter 2:20

Knowing this, that the trying of your faith worketh
patience. But let patience have her perfect work,
that ye may be perfect and entire, wanting nothing.
James 1:3-4

The Hammock, Joseph R. DeCamp, 1895

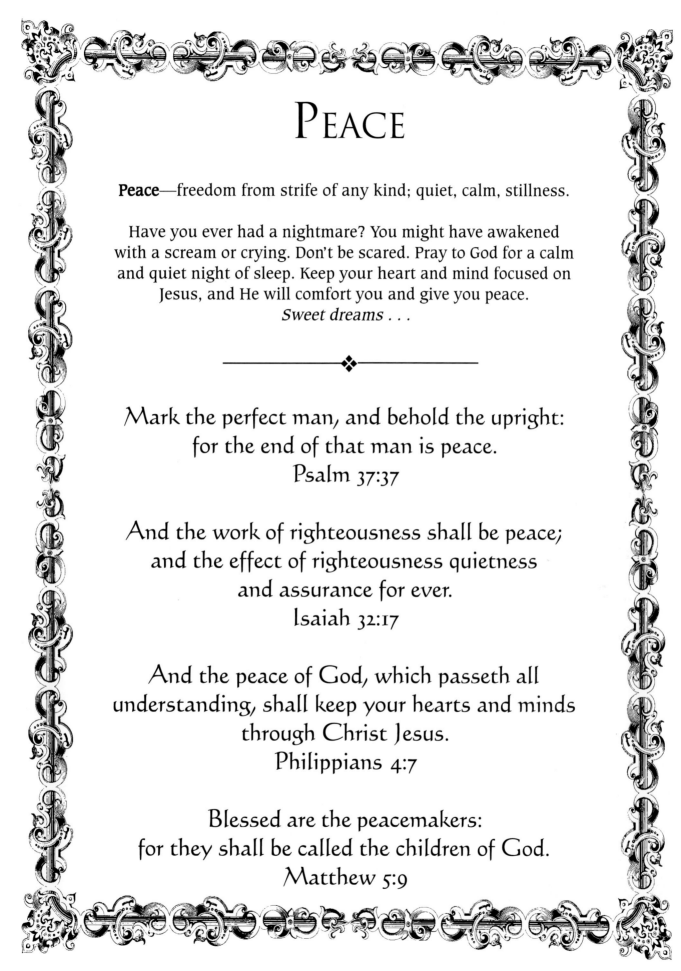

PEACE

Peace—freedom from strife of any kind; quiet, calm, stillness.

Have you ever had a nightmare? You might have awakened with a scream or crying. Don't be scared. Pray to God for a calm and quiet night of sleep. Keep your heart and mind focused on Jesus, and He will comfort you and give you peace.
Sweet dreams . . .

❖

Mark the perfect man, and behold the upright:
for the end of that man is peace.
Psalm 37:37

And the work of righteousness shall be peace;
and the effect of righteousness quietness
and assurance for ever.
Isaiah 32:17

And the peace of God, which passeth all
understanding, shall keep your hearts and minds
through Christ Jesus.
Philippians 4:7

Blessed are the peacemakers:
for they shall be called the children of God.
Matthew 5:9

Detail from *The Recall of the Gleaners,* Jules Breton, 1859

PERSEVERANCE

Perseverance—to continue steadily in doing something; never giving up what one has set out to do.

Have you ever quit something before you finished? It might have been cheerleading, or the baseball team. It's important not to become a quitter when things don't go your way. This might be an opportunity for you to build character, and persevere. You can make it!

❖

Be of good courage, and he shall strengthen your heart, all ye that hope in the Lord.
Psalm 31:24

Let us hold fast the profession of our faith without wavering;
(for he is faithful that promised;)
Hebrews 10:23

The Lord knoweth how to deliver the godly out of temptations, and to reserve the unjust unto the day of judgement to be punished.
2 Peter 2:9

For whatsoever is born of God overcometh the world: and this is the victory that overcometh the world, even our faith.
1 John 5:4

Poor People, André Collin, 1896

POVERTY

Poverty—lack of what is needed.

Sometimes you might want things that your parents can't afford to buy for you. Having a lot of material possessions doesn't make you richer than those who lack such items. Kids who get time and love from their parents are the real rich kids. Be satisfied with what God has given you, and He will bless you abundantly!

❖

He shall spare the poor and needy,
and shall save the souls of the needy.
Psalm 72:13

He will regard the prayers of the destitute,
and not despise their prayer.
Psalm 102:17

Sing unto the Lord, praise ye the Lord:
for he hath delivered the soul of the poor from
the hand of evildoers.
Jeremiah 20:13

Blessed are the poor in spirit:
for theirs is the kingdom of heaven.
Matthew 5:3

Detail from *Adoration of the Lamb,* Jan van Eyck, 1432

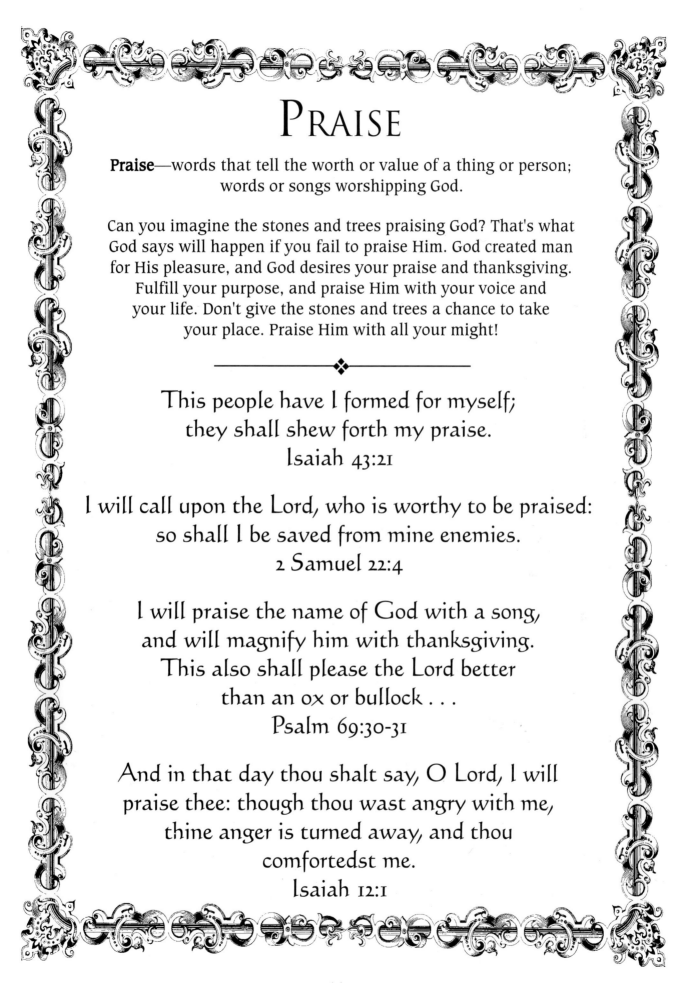

PRAISE

Praise—words that tell the worth or value of a thing or person; words or songs worshipping God.

Can you imagine the stones and trees praising God? That's what God says will happen if you fail to praise Him. God created man for His pleasure, and God desires your praise and thanksgiving. Fulfill your purpose, and praise Him with your voice and your life. Don't give the stones and trees a chance to take your place. Praise Him with all your might!

❖

This people have I formed for myself;
they shall shew forth my praise.
Isaiah 43:21

I will call upon the Lord, who is worthy to be praised:
so shall I be saved from mine enemies.
2 Samuel 22:4

I will praise the name of God with a song,
and will magnify him with thanksgiving.
This also shall please the Lord better
than an ox or bullock . . .
Psalm 69:30-31

And in that day thou shalt say, O Lord, I will
praise thee: though thou wast angry with me,
thine anger is turned away, and thou
comfortedst me.
Isaiah 12:1

The Angelus, Jean Francois Millet, 1855-57

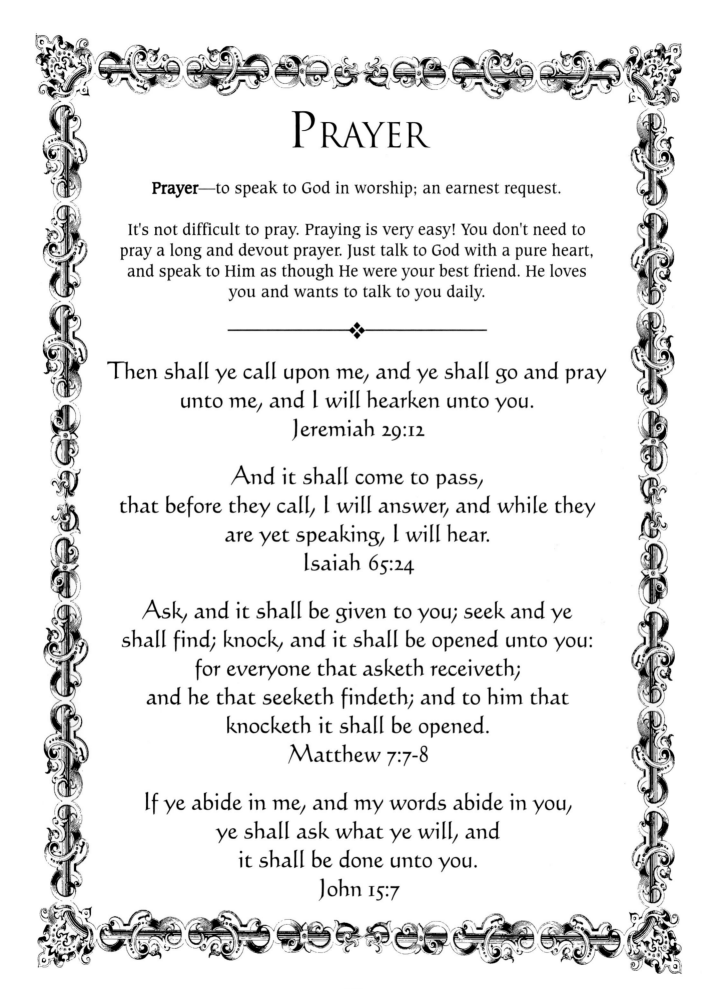

PRAYER

Prayer—to speak to God in worship; an earnest request.

It's not difficult to pray. Praying is very easy! You don't need to pray a long and devout prayer. Just talk to God with a pure heart, and speak to Him as though He were your best friend. He loves you and wants to talk to you daily.

❖

Then shall ye call upon me, and ye shall go and pray
unto me, and I will hearken unto you.
Jeremiah 29:12

And it shall come to pass,
that before they call, I will answer, and while they
are yet speaking, I will hear.
Isaiah 65:24

Ask, and it shall be given to you; seek and ye
shall find; knock, and it shall be opened unto you:
for everyone that asketh receiveth;
and he that seeketh findeth; and to him that
knocketh it shall be opened.
Matthew 7:7-8

If ye abide in me, and my words abide in you,
ye shall ask what ye will, and
it shall be done unto you.
John 15:7

La Discussion Politique, Emile Friant, 1889

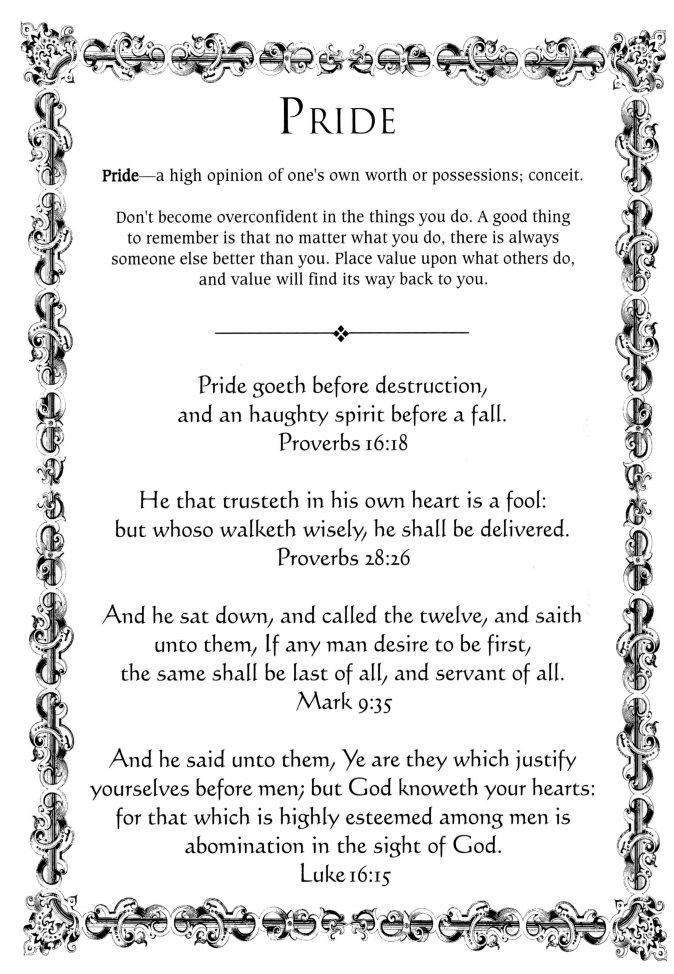

PRIDE

Pride—a high opinion of one's own worth or possessions; conceit.

Don't become overconfident in the things you do. A good thing to remember is that no matter what you do, there is always someone else better than you. Place value upon what others do, and value will find its way back to you.

❖

Pride goeth before destruction,
and an haughty spirit before a fall.
Proverbs 16:18

He that trusteth in his own heart is a fool:
but whoso walketh wisely, he shall be delivered.
Proverbs 28:26

And he sat down, and called the twelve, and saith
unto them, If any man desire to be first,
the same shall be last of all, and servant of all.
Mark 9:35

And he said unto them, Ye are they which justify
yourselves before men; but God knoweth your hearts:
for that which is highly esteemed among men is
abomination in the sight of God.
Luke 16:15

45

Madonna of the Chair, Raphael, circa 1518

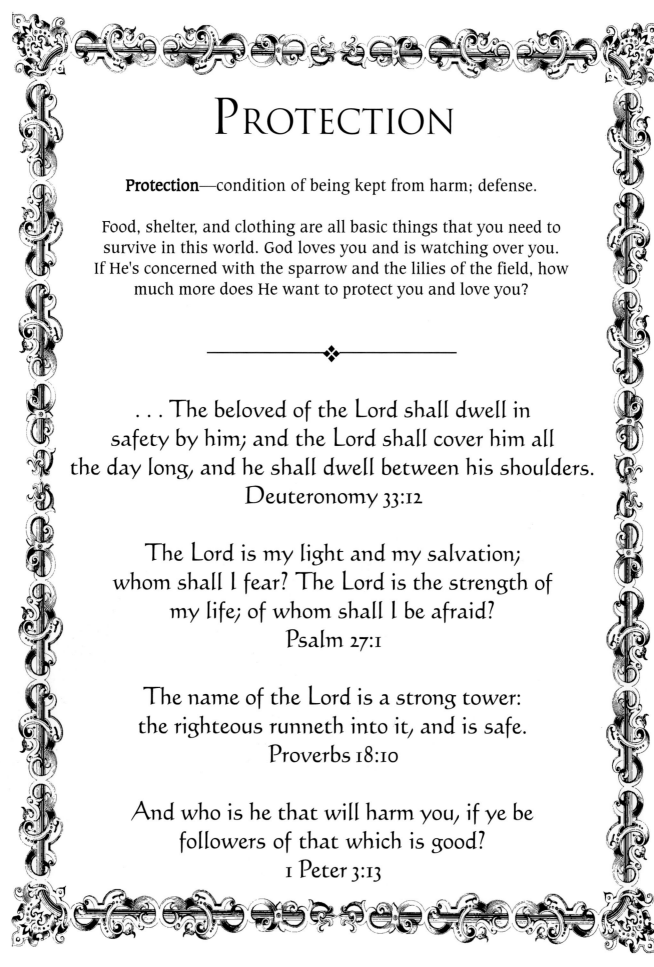

PROTECTION

Protection—condition of being kept from harm; defense.

Food, shelter, and clothing are all basic things that you need to survive in this world. God loves you and is watching over you. If He's concerned with the sparrow and the lilies of the field, how much more does He want to protect you and love you?

❖

. . . The beloved of the Lord shall dwell in safety by him; and the Lord shall cover him all the day long, and he shall dwell between his shoulders.
Deuteronomy 33:12

The Lord is my light and my salvation; whom shall I fear? The Lord is the strength of my life; of whom shall I be afraid?
Psalm 27:1

The name of the Lord is a strong tower: the righteous runneth into it, and is safe.
Proverbs 18:10

And who is he that will harm you, if ye be followers of that which is good?
1 Peter 3:13

Lo Spasimo di Sicilia, Raphael, circa 1516

SALVATION

Salvation—a free gift from God to all who believe.

It's as easy as ABC: Admit that you are a sinner.
Believe that Jesus died, and accept Him as your Lord,
and confess that He is your Savior.

❖

But as many as received him, to them gave he power
to become the sons of God, even to them that
believe on his name.
John 1:12

Jesus answered and said unto him,
Verily, Verily, I say unto thee, Except a man be born
again, he cannot see the kingdom of God.
John 3:3

For God so loved the world, that he gave his only
begotten Son, that whosoever believeth in him
should not perish, but have everlasting life.
John 3:16

For he hath made him to be sin for us, who
knew no sin; that we might be made the
righteousness of God in him.
2 Corinthians 5:21

Detail from *Tired,* William Merritt Chase, 1894

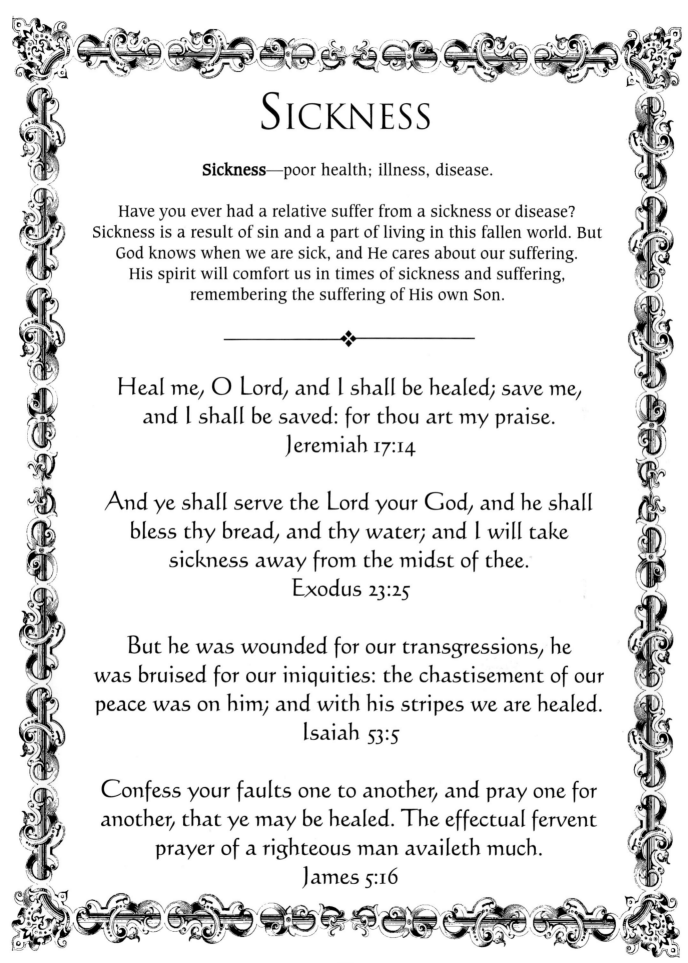

SICKNESS

Sickness—poor health; illness, disease.

Have you ever had a relative suffer from a sickness or disease? Sickness is a result of sin and a part of living in this fallen world. But God knows when we are sick, and He cares about our suffering. His spirit will comfort us in times of sickness and suffering, remembering the suffering of His own Son.

❖

Heal me, O Lord, and I shall be healed; save me, and I shall be saved: for thou art my praise.
Jeremiah 17:14

And ye shall serve the Lord your God, and he shall bless thy bread, and thy water; and I will take sickness away from the midst of thee.
Exodus 23:25

But he was wounded for our transgressions, he was bruised for our iniquities: the chastisement of our peace was on him; and with his stripes we are healed.
Isaiah 53:5

Confess your faults one to another, and pray one for another, that ye may be healed. The effectual fervent prayer of a righteous man availeth much.
James 5:16

Detail from *The Apostle Peter Denying Christ*, Rembrandt, 1660

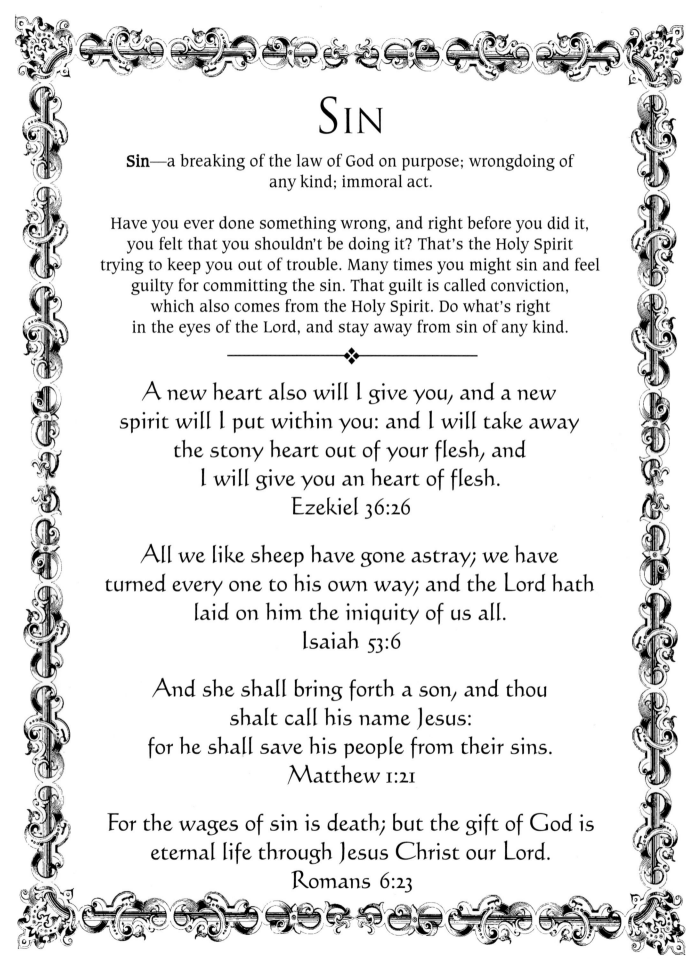

SIN

Sin—a breaking of the law of God on purpose; wrongdoing of any kind; immoral act.

Have you ever done something wrong, and right before you did it, you felt that you shouldn't be doing it? That's the Holy Spirit trying to keep you out of trouble. Many times you might sin and feel guilty for committing the sin. That guilt is called conviction, which also comes from the Holy Spirit. Do what's right in the eyes of the Lord, and stay away from sin of any kind.

❖

A new heart also will I give you, and a new spirit will I put within you: and I will take away the stony heart out of your flesh, and I will give you an heart of flesh.
Ezekiel 36:26

All we like sheep have gone astray; we have turned every one to his own way; and the Lord hath laid on him the iniquity of us all.
Isaiah 53:6

And she shall bring forth a son, and thou shalt call his name Jesus: for he shall save his people from their sins.
Matthew 1:21

For the wages of sin is death; but the gift of God is eternal life through Jesus Christ our Lord.
Romans 6:23

Detail from *The Prophet Jeremiah Lamenting the Destruction of Jerusalem*, Rembrandt, 1630

SORROW

Sorrow—grief, sadness, or regret; trouble; suffering misfortune.

Sometimes bad things happen. There's nothing wrong with feeling sad or crying. Sadness is a very normal emotion for human beings. But it's important not to dwell in your sorrow for a long time. God wants you to experience His joy in your life, and mourn for only a little while. Remember, joy comes in the morning!

❖

He shall call upon me, and I will answer him:
I will be with him in trouble;
I will deliver him, and honor him.
Psalm 91:15

This is my comfort in my affliction:
for thy word hath quickened me.
Psalm 119:50

Blessed are they that mourn: for they
shall be comforted.
Matthew 5:4

And ye now therefore have sorrow:
but I will see you again, and your heart shall rejoice,
and your joy no man taketh from you.
John 16:22

Don Manuel Osorio DeZũniga, Francisco Goya

TEMPTATION

Temptation—to appeal strongly to; attract; to induce or persuade.

Have you ever given in to peer pressure? Pressure from friends to do things that are wrong in God's eyes is the biggest form of temptation that you face. Remember, obey and serve God, not people. Don't go with the flow to be accepted, because then you'll just be considered average. Stand your ground, and do what's right, because that's special!

❖

Ye are of God, little children, and have overcome them: because greater is he that is in you, than he that is in the world.
1 John 4:4

Submit yourselves therefore to God.
Resist the devil and he will flee from you.
James 4:7

Above all, taking the shield of faith, where-with ye shall be able to quench all the fiery darts of the wicked.
Ephesians 6:16

For in that he himself hath suffered being tempted, he is able to succour them that are tempted.
Hebrews 2:18

Detail from *"Do This in Memory of Me!"* Istuan Csok, 1890

UNITY

Unity—the fact, quality, or condition of being one; oneness.

Have you ever run in a three-legged race? You and your partner had to run together in order to keep that middle leg in step with the others. Without unity you would stumble, fall, and lose the race. God has called you to walk in unity with those around you. Stay away from disagreements and conflict which will surely cause you to stumble and fall in the race of life.

❖

For then will I turn to the people a pure language, that they may all call upon the name of the Lord, to serve him with one consent.
Zephaniah 3:9

That they all may be one; as thou, Father, art in me, and I in thee, that they also may be one in us: that the world may believe that thou hast sent me.
John 17:21

Fulfill ye my joy, that ye be likeminded, having the same love, being of one accord, of one mind.
Philippians 2:2

By this shall all men know that ye are my disciples, if ye have love one to another.
John 13:35

Ince Hall Madonna, Jan van Eyck, 1433

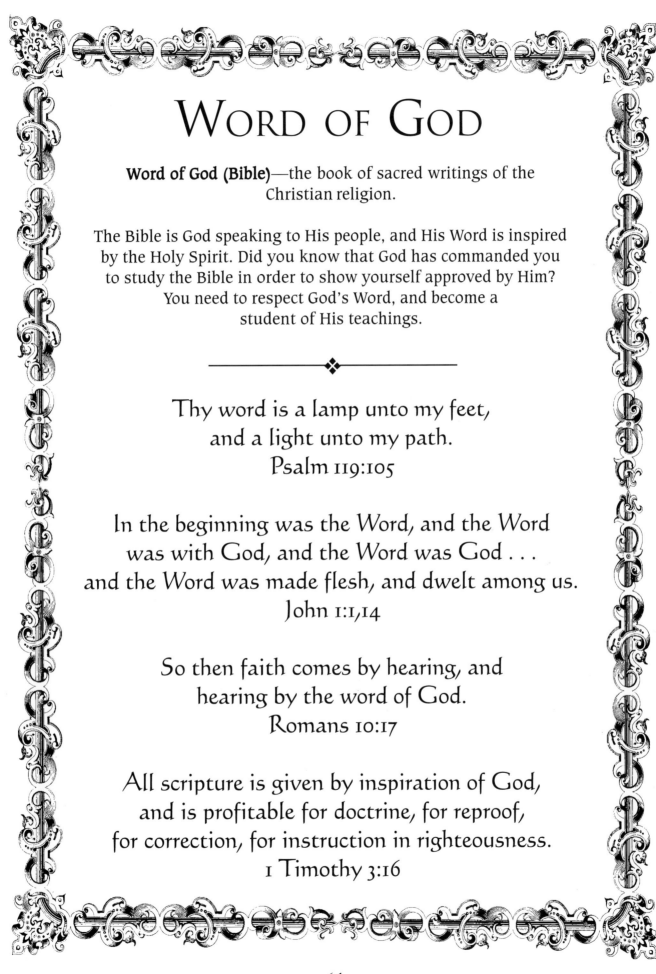

WORD OF GOD

Word of God (Bible)—the book of sacred writings of the Christian religion.

The Bible is God speaking to His people, and His Word is inspired by the Holy Spirit. Did you know that God has commanded you to study the Bible in order to show yourself approved by Him? You need to respect God's Word, and become a student of His teachings.

❖

Thy word is a lamp unto my feet,
and a light unto my path.
Psalm 119:105

In the beginning was the Word, and the Word
was with God, and the Word was God . . .
and the Word was made flesh, and dwelt among us.
John 1:1,14

So then faith comes by hearing, and
hearing by the word of God.
Romans 10:17

All scripture is given by inspiration of God,
and is profitable for doctrine, for reproof,
for correction, for instruction in righteousness.
1 Timothy 3:16

LIST OF ART AND ARTISTS

Anger:
LaLutte(Wrestling), Emile Frian, 1889

Children:
Detail from *Sunlight*, Frank Benson, 1902

Comfort:
Mother and Child, J. Alden Weir, 1891

Courage:
Saint George and the Dragon, Raphael, 1504-1505

Faith:
The Angel Stopping Abraham from Sacrificing Isaac to God, Rembrandt, 1635

Fear:
The Fire, Jean-Pierre Alexandre Antigna, 1850

Forgiveness:
Detail from *The Return of the Prodigal Son*, Rembrandt, 17th Century

Grace:
Detail from *The Adoration of the Shepherds*, Giorgione (Venice), circa 1505

Guidance:
Detail from *Advice to a Young Artist*, Honoré Daumier, circa 1860

Hope:
Sketch for *Soldiers Distributing Bread*, Isidore Pils, circa 1850

Humility:
Holy Family with the Lamb, Raphael, circa 1505

Joy:
Detail from *Breezing Up*, Winslow Homer, 1876

Love for Others:
The Artist's Family, Renoir, 1896

Patience:
The Little Cook, Pierre Edouard Frère, 1858

Peace:
The Hammock, Joseph R. DeCamp, 1895

Perseverance:
Detail from *The Recall of the Gleaners*, Jules Breton, 1859

Poverty:
The Beggar, Jules-Bastien Lepage, 1870

Praise:
Detail from *Adoration of the Lamb*, Jan van Eyck, 1432

Prayer:
The Angelus, Jean Francois Millet, 1855-57

Pride:
La Discussion Politique, Emile Friant, 1889

Protection:
Madonna della Sedia or *Madonna of the Chair*, Raphael, circa 1518

Salvation:
Lo Spasimo di Sicilia, Raphael, circa 1516

Sickness:
Detail from *Tired*, William Merritt Chase, 1894

Sin:
Detail from *The Apostle Peter Denying Christ*, Rembrandt, 1660

Sorrow:
Detail from *The Prophet Jeremiah Lamenting the Destruction of Jerusalem*,
Rembrandt, 1630

Temptation:
Don Manuel Osorio DeZũniga, Francisco Goya

Unity:
Detail from *"Do This in Memory of Me!"* Istuan Csok, 1890

Word of God:
Ince Hall Madonna, Jan van Eyck, 1433